1-2-3, Special Like Me!

BY Lisa Kay Hauser
AND Philip Dale Smith
ART BY Donna Brooks

Golden Anchor Press

We dedicate this book to all teachers—especially the following:

Eileen Downs and **Alta Russell,** my kindergarten and first grade teachers at McKinley School in Eau Claire, WI, reached far beyond the basics of education and into the heart of the child. They infected me with an excitement for learning that carried me all through my school years. They helped me find my "specialness," encouraged my curiosity, delighted in my precocious vocabulary, and encouraged me to read ahead of the class. Thanks, ladies. You made a difference. —LISA KAY HAUSER

Jennie Ashby, the ultimate student-sensitive teacher. She helped me believe I could achieve. Others nudging me along were: **Mildred Earle, Evelyn Lindsey, A.T. Ross, Hilda Durham, Peggy Parrish, Tom and Hope Neathamer, Geneva Kutzner, Dencil Vincent, Ethel Mercer,** and **Howard Shaver.** —PHILIP DALE SMITH

A.Y. Hodge, band director at Webster Co. (KY) High School, brought out the best in us and led us to honors only dreamed of—even a trip to play in the Mardi Gras parade. I still feel his influence in my life. I also dedicate this book to teacher **Sandy Woodard** of Chandler Elementary School in Corydon, KY, and to the enthusiastic and cooperative students at that school who modeled for the children in this book. —DONNA BROOKS

Publisher's Cataloging-in-Publication

(Provided by Cassidy Cataloguing Services)

Hauser, Lisa Kay.
  1-2-3, special like me! / by Lisa Kay Hauser and
Philip Dale Smith ; illustrated by Donna Brooks.
  — Tacoma, WA : Golden Anchor Press, 2004.
    p. ; cm.
    Audience: 4–7 years
    ISBN 1–886864–17–9

  1. Self-esteem in children—Juvenile fiction.
  2. Respect for persons—Juvenile fiction.
  3. Counting—Juvenile fiction.   4. [Stories in rhyme.]
  I. Smith, Philip Dale. II. Brooks, Donna. III. Title.

P .3 .H386 2004   2003104216
[E] —dc21   0401

Published by

Golden Anchor Press
Tacoma, WA 98444

Portions of the text first appeared in Lisa Kay Hauser's children's newspaper column in The Independent Register, Brodhead, WI, © 2001 by Lisa Kay Hauser.

The art for each picture is an original oil painting on canvas, which is color separated and reproduced in full color.

This book is printed on acid-free paper
(So your children can pass it on to their children)

Printed in China by Leo Paper

Cover design by Foster and Foster
Fairfield, Iowa

Interior typesetting by Desktop Miracles, Inc.
Stowe, Vermont

Golden Anchor Press books are available at special discount for bulk purchases for fund-raising efforts, sales promotions, and educational use. Note: Special editions, prints, excerpts, etc., can be created to your specification.

Check these Web sites:
www.goldenanchorpress.com
www.everykidawinner.com

One little tulip pushed her way
Toward the sun on a bright spring day.
Nodded her head to the bluebirds high
And wished that she knew how to fly.

Two little bluebirds flitted and flew
Up to the trees in a sky of blue.
They watched the clouds billow away
And wished to fly that high some day.

Three little clouds went floating by
Out across the noonday sky.
They looked down on the earth below
And wished that they could go so low.

four little ladybugs flew in a line,
And landed on a flowering vine.
There they looked out on the view
And wished that they were different, too.

Five little daffodils raised their heads,
Stretched their leaves from earthy beds.
They could not leap, nor crawl, or fly
And so they all began to cry.

Six little caterpillars poked about
And for themselves began to doubt.
They saw the creatures scampering past
And wished they too could go so fast.

Seven little squirrels with fluffy tails
Played along the old fence rails.
Their game came to a sudden stop
To watch a different kind of hop.

Eight little rabbits ran and chased,
Wiggling their noses as they raced.
They watched the children all go by
And wished to dance, but didn't try.

Nine little girls with soft curled tresses
Whirled about in dress-up dresses,
Giggled and spun in twists and twirls—
Happy, laughing, little girls.

Ten little boys with line and pole,
Off to try the fishing hole,
Romping, shouting, making noise—
Silly, funny, little boys.

A wise old owl in a sycamore tree
Saw it all from his perch, you see.
He called the animals, birds and flowers,
He called the clouds down to his bower.

"You're all quite wrong to wish for things
That aren't yours—not what life brings."
The old owl fluffed his ruffled feathers,
And settled down among the heathers.

"You shouldn't wish for what you're not.
Instead, be glad for what you've got!
You bluebirds have the gift of song.
Why would you think that this is wrong?"

"You fluffy, furry squirrels and rabbits
Have no need for dancing habits.
And slow caterpillars, don't you know
You'll soon fly where the butterflies go?"

"You should be happy, ladybugs,
You weren't created to be slugs.
You could've been an ugly creature,
Without spots as your best feature."

"Daffodils and your tulip friend,
Without the clouds the rain to send,
You'd shrivel up like weary prunes.
Your lives would be in total ruins."

"When the children wandered by
Not one of them sat down to cry
Because they couldn't bloom or blossom
Or turn themselves into a 'possum."

The owl turned his mighty back
Toward the shamed, ungrateful pack.
"How sad I feel for you today,
You make me tired. Now go away!"

Ten little boys with strings of fish
Got their springtime fishing wish.
They went home with tales to tell
About how fishing went so well.

Nine little girls tumbled in a heap,
Tired of dancing, ready to sleep.
They went home to cozy beds,
Pillows ready for their heads.

Eight little rabbits found their burrows,
Underneath a field of furrows.
They each admired the others' fluff,
And knew that it was quite enough.

Seven little squirrels bounced down a path
As they went home to take a bath.
All together, their fur they brushed
Until it shone in the twilight hush.

Six little caterpillars wiggled away,
To dream about a coming day,
When out of nowhere nature brings
Their brilliant gem-stone colored wings.

Five little daffodils fluffed their crowns.
From roots embedded in the ground.
Proud they are of their beauty now,
And thankfully their heads they bow.

Four little ladybugs flew away home
For there was now no need to roam.
Lovingly they checked their dots.
Carefully they polished their spots.

Three little clouds watched the earth below.
When flowers need rain, the clouds will know.
They see now that they're needed, too,
Their sweet rain and the morning dew.

Two little bluebirds found their nest—
Ready for a good night's rest.
Tomorrow they will sing their song
From the trees where they belong.

One little tulip stood up tall.
She will watch them one and all.
And she'll remember every day
To be herself in every way.

The moon beamed down upon the world
At all the beauty there unfurled.
It smiled upon the field and wood,
At all of nature, right and good.

A note to parents, grandparents, and others who care about children

When you read to children, it tells them that books are important, that reading is important, and most of all, that they're important! And what a wonderful way to bond generations! You connect, you share, and you create a reservoir of common knowledge and mutual memories.

Reading with your children can be the most rewarding part of your day, whether it's part of your bedtime ritual, a morning, or an afternoon activity. There's nothing sweeter than cuddling your little one. When you include a book in that experience it becomes even more precious. As the children grow, they become more involved in the experience. As they share in the reading, and together you discuss the story, you open their minds to the world around them. Your children learn that through books they can meet fascinating people, go to exciting and mysterious places, and have marvelous adventures.

The development of a hunger to read best begins when children are small—the ideal time to take a youngster on a romp through this book. Several factors make *1-2-3, Special Like Me!* a treasured story. They include the trip from one to ten and back again, the brilliant pictures, the colorful characters, and the lesson that the child and all others are special, with their own individual gifts, talents, and life opportunities.

Here are suggestions to enrich your shared reading time:

- **First, read the book**—letting it take you and the children along on the journey—with the inevitable interruptions your little ones add. Have fun!

- **Now go back and look for interesting things you didn't see the first time.**
  - Talk about the colors on the page: the red tulip, the yellow daffodils, the brown squirrels
  - Count the rabbits and the caterpillars
  - Ask questions. "How many cows are on the page with the three clouds?" Or, "On the page with eight rabbits, three are on the grass. How many are on the path?" And, "What did Owl say the caterpillars would soon get to do?"

- **In future readings respond to the child's excitement as the story unfolds.** Let them tell about parts they like. Help with new words. Continue to ask questions— for example, "Why are the five daffodils sad?" Listen to their answers.

Such activities will greatly enhance the child's comprehension and enjoyment of what they are read and see. Have a happy time!

—*Lisa Kay Hauser & Philip Dale Smith*

P.S. Go to www.goldenanchorpress.com to see our other children's picture books,
the award-winning novel, *Turn Back Time,* and its sequels.
Note also the YA novel, *Secrets of Rebel Cave.*
Get your free copy of the special report, **Seven Keys to Family Reading Fun.**